Happy Birthday, Belly Button!

For Henry and Wesley
and their belly buttons too—K.D.

• • •

To my favorite belly buttons Alexander and Nicolas.
Para o umbigo mais novo da família, George; e Emilia.
To Felix and Olivia—L.N.P.

Text copyright © 2023 Kalli Dakos
Illustrations copyright © 2023 Luciana Navarro Powell

Published in 2023 by Amicus Ink, an imprint of Amicus
P.O. Box 227, Mankato MN 56002
www.amicuspublishing.us

All rights reserved. No part of the contents of this book may be reproduced by any means without the written permission of the publisher.

Library of Congress Cataloging-in-Publication Data
Names: Dakos, Kalli, author. | Powell, Luciana Navarro, illustrator.
Title: Happy birthday, belly button! / by Kalli Dakos ; illustrated by Luciana Navarro Powell.
Description: Mankato, Minnesota : Amicus Ink, 2023. | Audience: Ages 2–5.
Summary: "An exuberant child celebrates being one year older, calling out body parts from head to toe (don't forget the belly button!) that have grown since their last birthday"—Provided by publisher.
Identifiers: LCCN 2022001163 (print) | LCCN 2022001164 (ebook)
| ISBN 9781681527512 (hardcover) | ISBN 9781681528687 (paperback)
| ISBN 9781681527529 (pdf)
Subjects: CYAC: Stories in rhyme. | Human body—Fiction. | Growth—Fiction.
| Birthdays—Fiction. | LCGFT: Picture books. | Stories in rhyme.
Classification: LCC PZ8.3.D1395 Hap 2023 (print) | LCC PZ8.3.D1395 (ebook) | DDC [E]—dc23
LC record available at https://lccn.loc.gov/2022001163
LC ebook record available at https://lccn.loc.gov/2022001164

Edited by Rebecca Glaser
Art direction and design by Catherine Berthiaume and Lori Bye

First edition 9 8 7 6 5 4 3 2 1
Printed in China

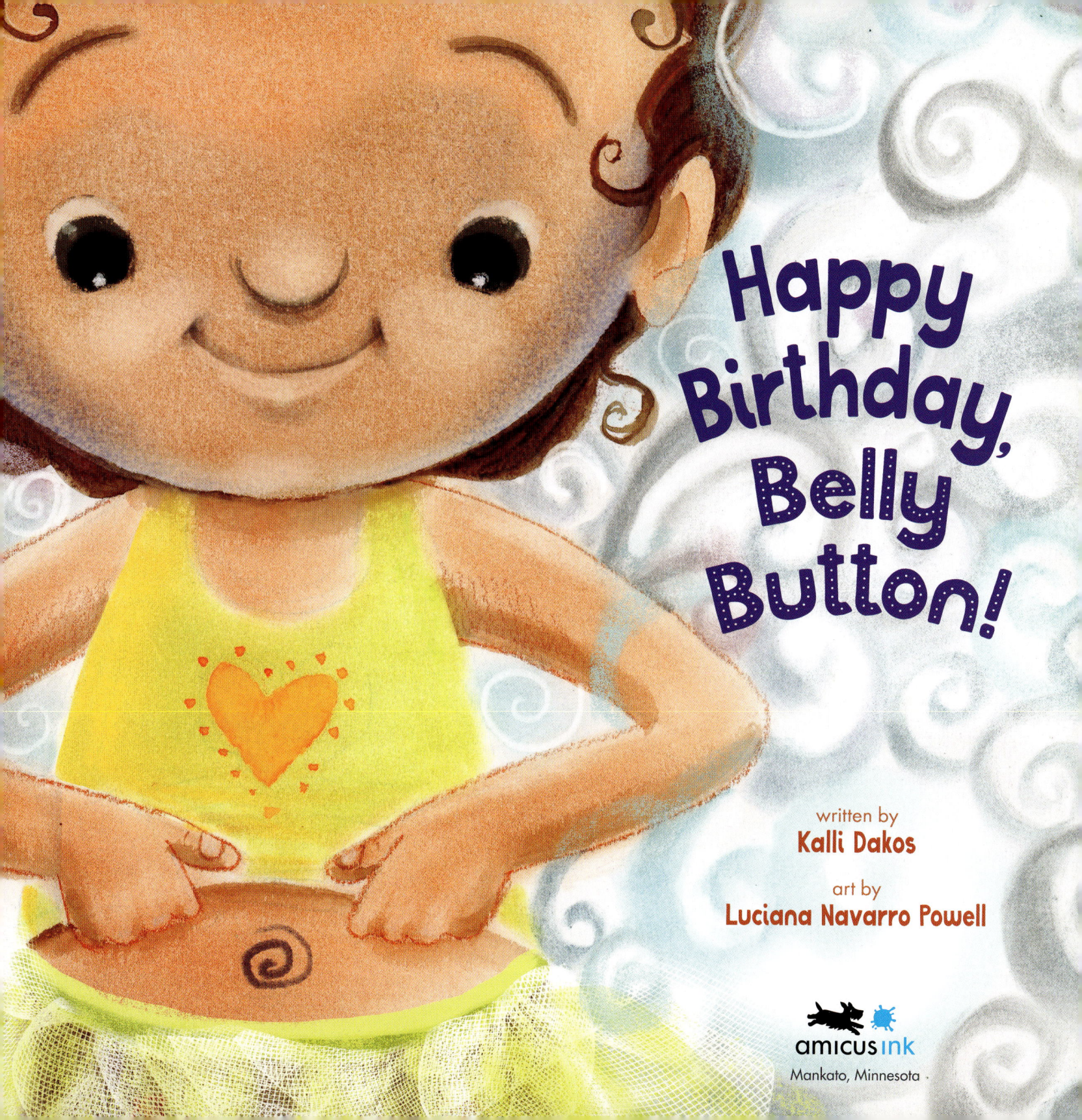

For one long year,
I grew and grew.

My arms and legs
and my
belly button too!

In three hundred days and sixty-five more,

Now I need a bigger chair because I have a bigger seat,

and I need bigger socks 'cause I have bigger feet.

My tummy is older and so is my nose.

There's a lot more ME

when I wiggle my toes.

My brain is larger
and getting quite wide.
I grew a bigger head,
so it could fit inside.

My head is sprouting a lot more curly hair, and I need a larger size in . . .

My skeleton dances as my bones all cheer,

"Hip! Hip! Hooray! It's been a great year!"

My funny bone laughs, "I'm sillier today!"

My thumbs are wiggling.
"Look how large we grew!

Here's a thumbs-up,
and a happy birthday too!"

"I've grown much longer," says my little right pinkie.

"But I'm still the smallest, and this is quite . . . stinky!"

My mouth is huge when I open it to shout,

and my tongue is
looooooooong,
when I want to stick it out.

My ears are bigger,

and so are my cheeks,

because I've been growing

for **fifty-two weeks!**

It's time for a PARTY,
and we'll all be there,

my cheeks and my lips
and every strand of hair.

Today is my birthday, and I'm feeling brand new.
Happy birthday to me and to my **belly button** too!